# The MAIDEN on the MOOR

MARILYN SINGER

*The*

# MAIDEN

*on the*

# MOOR

ILLUSTRATED BY

# TROY HOWELL

MORROW JUNIOR BOOKS
NEW YORK

*A Maiden on the Moor*

*A maiden on the moor lay,*
*On the moor lay,*
*Seven nights full, seven nights full.*
*A maiden on the moor lay,*
*On the moor lay,*
*Seven nights full and a day.*

*Good was her meat,*
*What was her meat?*
*The primrose and the——*
*The primrose and the——*
*Good was her meat,*
*What was her meat?*
*The primrose and the violet.*

Good was her drink,
What was her drink?
The cold water of the—
The cold water of the—
Good was her drink,
What was her drink?
The cold water of the wellspring.

Good was her bower,
What was her bower?
The red rose and the—
The red rose and the—
Good was her bower,
What was her bower?
The red rose and the lily flower.

Anonymous
*Adapted from medieval English verse
by Marilyn Singer*

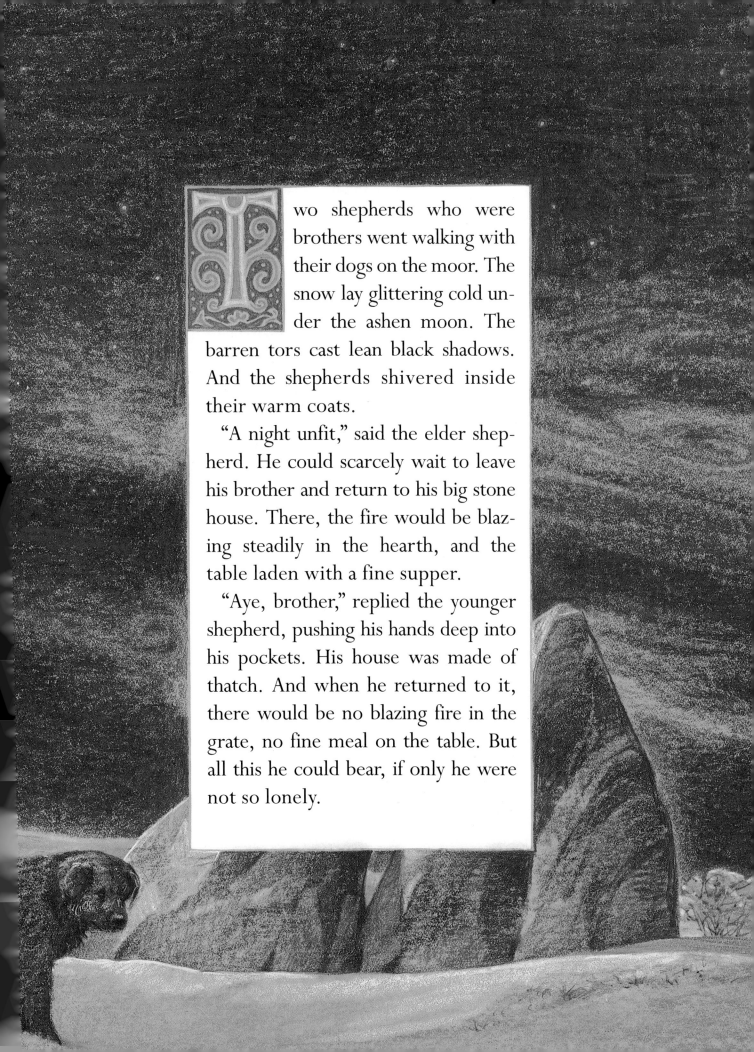

wo shepherds who were brothers went walking with their dogs on the moor. The snow lay glittering cold under the ashen moon. The barren tors cast lean black shadows. And the shepherds shivered inside their warm coats.

"A night unfit," said the elder shepherd. He could scarcely wait to leave his brother and return to his big stone house. There, the fire would be blazing steadily in the hearth, and the table laden with a fine supper.

"Aye, brother," replied the younger shepherd, pushing his hands deep into his pockets. His house was made of thatch. And when he returned to it, there would be no blazing fire in the grate, no fine meal on the table. But all this he could bear, if only he were not so lonely.

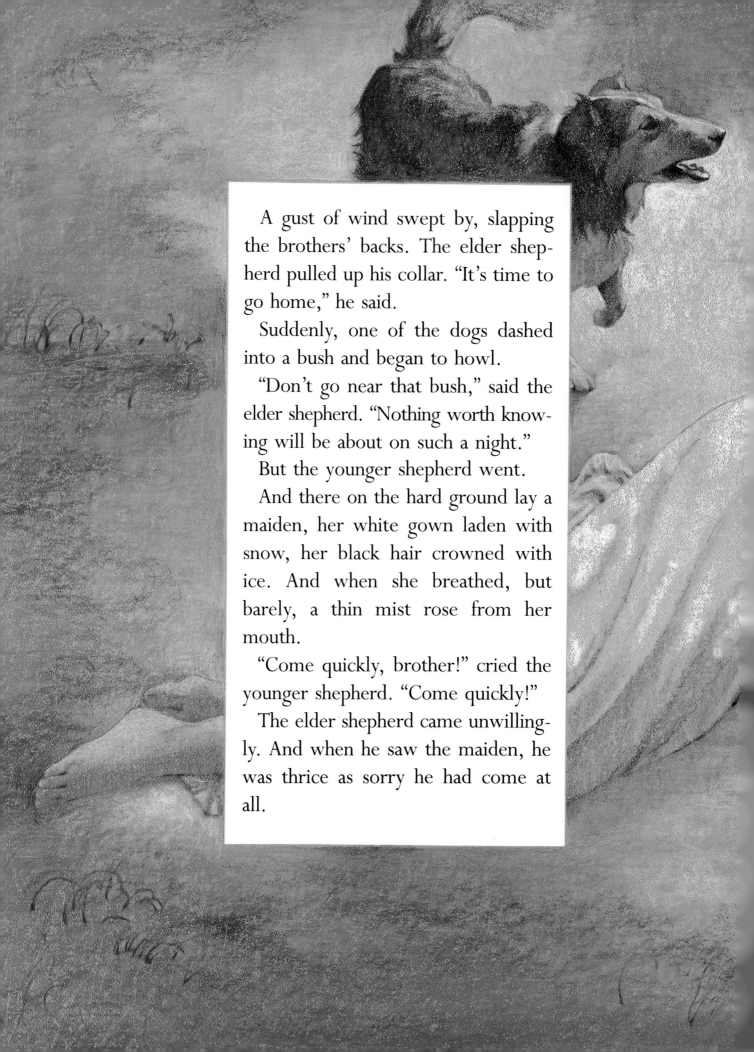

A gust of wind swept by, slapping the brothers' backs. The elder shepherd pulled up his collar. "It's time to go home," he said.

Suddenly, one of the dogs dashed into a bush and began to howl.

"Don't go near that bush," said the elder shepherd. "Nothing worth knowing will be about on such a night."

But the younger shepherd went.

And there on the hard ground lay a maiden, her white gown laden with snow, her black hair crowned with ice. And when she breathed, but barely, a thin mist rose from her mouth.

"Come quickly, brother!" cried the younger shepherd. "Come quickly!"

The elder shepherd came unwillingly. And when he saw the maiden, he was thrice as sorry he had come at all.

"We must bring her to where it is warm. Let us go to your house at once," his brother proposed.

The elder shepherd shook his head. "We know nothing of her. She may well be an enchanter. She may be bewitched. I do not want her in my house."

But his brother was not afraid. "Then help me take her to my home," he said. "Chilly though it may be, it is warmer than this frozen moor."

But again the elder shepherd refused. "Your brain is as soft as your heart, brother. I will not help you."

"Then I must carry her alone," said the younger man. Wrapping the maiden in his sheepskin coat, he lifted her in his arms and set off for home, his three dogs following close behind.

"Fool!" the elder shepherd called after him. He turned and ran to his big stone house without looking back.

The maiden was light, but the way was long and bitterly cold. The younger shepherd's bones ached and his teeth rattled in his head as he trudged across the moor.

When he reached his cottage, his arms were numb and his legs trembled. He laid the maiden on his bed and gazed down at her. She gleamed so pale in the moonlight, he could scarcely believe she was real.

The wet muzzle of a dog against his hand shook him from his wonderment, and quickly he set to work. He covered the maiden with a flannel robe. He tucked blankets of sheepskin around her. And although he usually parceled out his wood with care, that night he built a grand fire in the grate and began to heat some gruel.

As he worked, he sang:

*"Good was her bower,*
*What was her bower?*
*The red rose and the—*
*The red rose and the—*
*Good was her bower,*
*What was her bower?*
*The red rose and the lily flower."*

The dogs watched silently.

When he was finished eating, he stretched himself before the hearth and slept.

And one by one, the dogs crept quietly onto the maiden's bed.

The biggest lay at her feet.

The next, at her head.

And the smallest, whose brown eyes danced and whose fur was as golden as an autumn leaf, rested against the maiden's side, her head on the maiden's heart.

So they spent the night.

And in the morning, before the sun rose and before the shepherd stirred in front of the cold grate, the dogs slid softly from the bed and waited by the door.

For six days and nights, the maiden lay in the younger shepherd's house. She did not speak. She did not eat. She did not awaken.

In the evenings, when he returned from his flocks, he sat at her side. At first he, too, was silent. Then he began to talk of his life as a shepherd, his love for the moors. He told her how in the spring the pale yellow flowers perched like birds on the broom bushes. He spoke of summer's shining days, its sea of heather, purple and green. But he did not speak of the sadness in his heart. At evening's end, he bid the maiden good night and took his place by the hearth. And as he lay there dreaming, the dogs crept onto the maiden's bed and slept there, quiet and still.

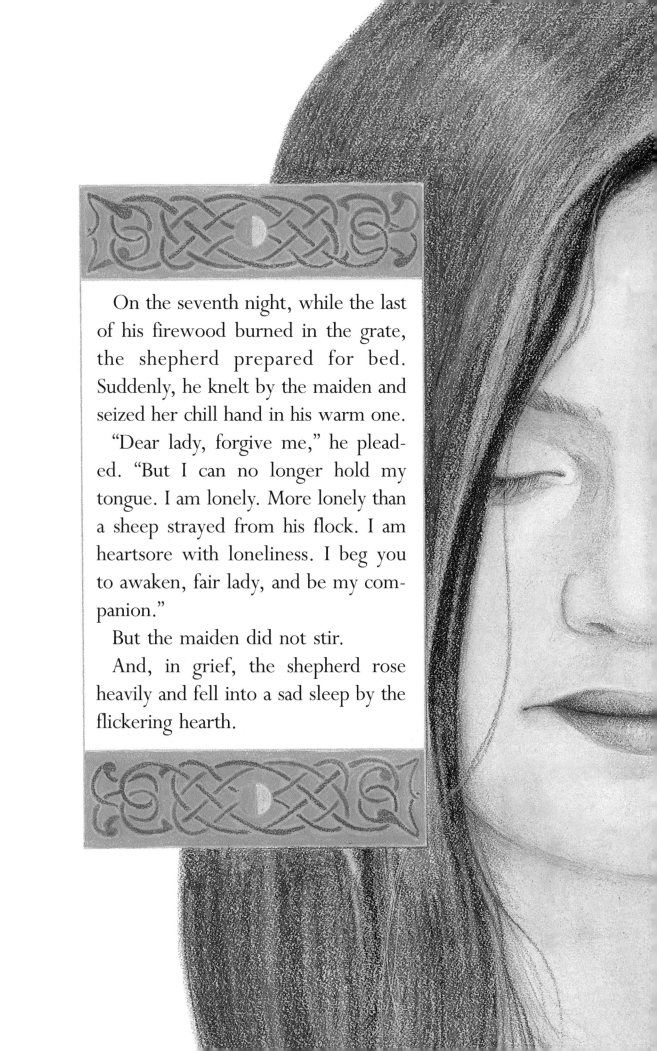

On the seventh night, while the last of his firewood burned in the grate, the shepherd prepared for bed. Suddenly, he knelt by the maiden and seized her chill hand in his warm one.

"Dear lady, forgive me," he pleaded. "But I can no longer hold my tongue. I am lonely. More lonely than a sheep strayed from his flock. I am heartsore with loneliness. I beg you to awaken, fair lady, and be my companion."

But the maiden did not stir.

And, in grief, the shepherd rose heavily and fell into a sad sleep by the flickering hearth.

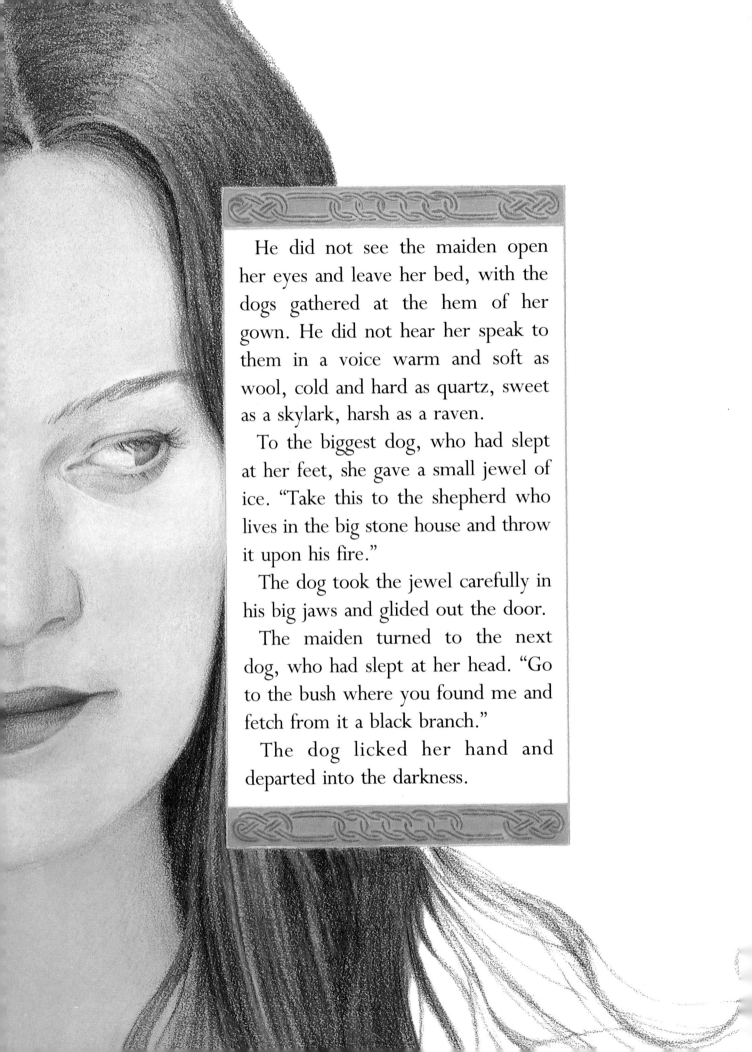

He did not see the maiden open her eyes and leave her bed, with the dogs gathered at the hem of her gown. He did not hear her speak to them in a voice warm and soft as wool, cold and hard as quartz, sweet as a skylark, harsh as a raven.

To the biggest dog, who had slept at her feet, she gave a small jewel of ice. "Take this to the shepherd who lives in the big stone house and throw it upon his fire."

The dog took the jewel carefully in his big jaws and glided out the door.

The maiden turned to the next dog, who had slept at her head. "Go to the bush where you found me and fetch from it a black branch."

The dog licked her hand and departed into the darkness.

Last, she spoke to the smallest dog, whose golden head had lain against her heart. "Not yet, my friend, but soon I will ask a favor of you. For now, let us bide together."

And so they waited.

Soon, the biggest dog returned, a coal from the hearth of the big stone house in his mouth.

"Well done," the maiden said, patting his head.

Then the next dog returned, carrying a bare black branch.

"Well done," the maiden told him, laying it upon her pillow.

Then she turned to the smallest dog. "Come." She beckoned, and together they went out onto the moor.

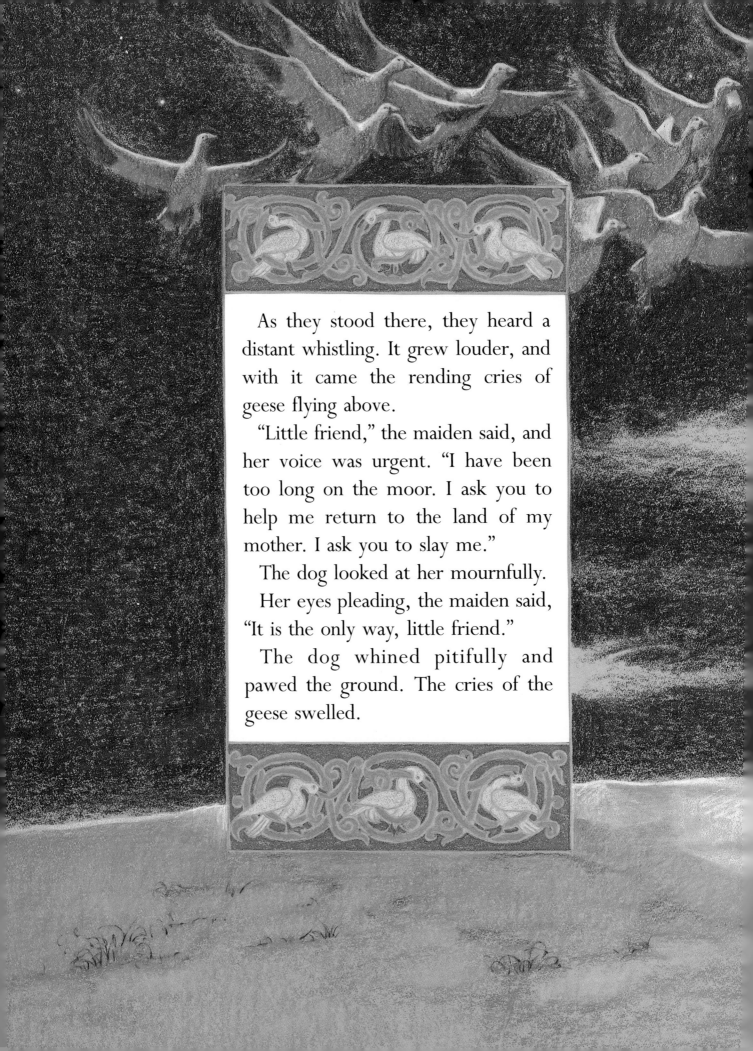

As they stood there, they heard a distant whistling. It grew louder, and with it came the rending cries of geese flying above.

"Little friend," the maiden said, and her voice was urgent. "I have been too long on the moor. I ask you to help me return to the land of my mother. I ask you to slay me."

The dog looked at her mournfully.

Her eyes pleading, the maiden said, "It is the only way, little friend."

The dog whined pitifully and pawed the ground. The cries of the geese swelled.

"I beg of you. Do it swiftly." She sank to her knees in a circle of moonlight.

And the dog seized her by the throat and slew her.

Then the dog threw back her head and howled. And the geese joined in plaintively.

But the white heap at her paws stirred.

Frightened, the dog leaped backward. She saw before her two white wings and a long white neck, graceful as birch branches, then two eyes, dark and ancient as the moor.

It was a snow goose.

She blinked once. Then, with a cry that was echoed by the flock of geese above, she raised her great wings and soared north into the starry night.

On the ground below, gazing at her path in the sky, was a young woman whose brown eyes danced and whose hair was as golden as an autumn leaf.

The next morning, the younger shepherd was awakened by a crashing at his door.

"Let me in! Let me in!" a voice bellowed.

He opened the door, and in stumbled his brother.

"What is the matter?" he asked.

"My hearth, my hearth. It is all ice!" the older shepherd cried.

"Scrape it and light a fire," replied his brother.

"I cannot! Come help me! Help me!"

The younger shepherd pulled on his boots, and with no time to glance at the maiden's bed or to notice his silent dogs, he went with his brother to the big stone house.

There, he found his brother's wife and children crying and shivering. The fire was gone, and the great hearth was filled with ice. Ice hung from the roof. Ice grew from the floor. Ice rose up the chimney.

The younger shepherd took an axe and chopped at the ice, but it would not break. He lit a torch and held it to the ice, but it would not melt.

"I can do nothing," he said at last.

"It is bewitched!" screamed his brother's wife.

And so it was.

And so it remained.

When the younger shepherd returned to his cottage, he saw that the maiden was gone. On the bed where she had lain was a black branch. Gone, too, was the smallest dog. He looked everywhere for them, but they were not to be found.

Clasping the branch in his hands, he sank onto the bed and began to weep. His tears fell on the bare wood, and it began to bud, then burst into fragrant scarlet bloom. Flowers twined about the bed, clung to the rafters, covered the ceiling. They encircled the hearth, in which a fire now blazed cheerfully. At last, the flowers started to frame the doorway. The younger shepherd turned his head to watch them, and there stood a golden-haired young woman.

She came to him and dried his eyes. "I will be your companion," she said, "now and for all time."

The younger shepherd took her hands in his and embraced her. And as the two dogs ran merry circles around their feet, his heart leaped light as a lamb in May.

*To Michael O'Donnell and John Quimby*
—M. S.

*To Daniel and Danelle*
—T. H.

Prismacolor pencils on museum board were used for the full-color illustrations.
The text type is 18-point Perpetua.
Text copyright © 1995 by Marilyn Singer
Illustrations copyright © 1995 by Troy Howell

Printed in Singapore at Tien Wah Press.
1 2 3 4 5 6 7 8 9 10
Library of Congress Cataloging-in-Publication Data
Singer, Marilyn.
The maiden on the moor / Marilyn Singer; illustrated by Troy Howell. p. cm.
Summary: A tale inspired by a medieval ballad in which a rich brother and a poor
brother find a beautiful maiden on the moor on a cold winter night.
ISBN 0-688-08674-8 (trade)—ISBN 0-688-08675-6 (library)
[1. Ballads, English. 2. Folklore—England.] I. Howell, Troy, ill. II. Title.
PZ8.1.S57835Mai 1994 398.2'1'0942—dc19 89-2985 CIP AC